Tractor Mac
HARVEST TIME
written and illustrated by Billy Steers

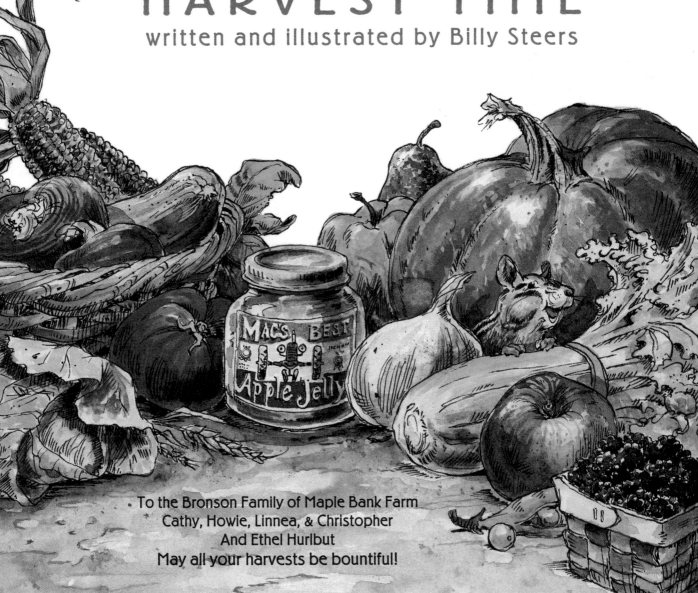

To the Bronson Family of Maple Bank Farm
Cathy, Howie, Linnea, & Christopher
And Ethel Hurlbut
May all your harvests be bountiful!

Tractor Mac noticed it first. The nights were getting cooler, the corn was ready to harvest, and the huge orange "Pumpkin Patch" signs were set up across the road from Stony Meadow Farm.

It was time for the neighboring farm's Pumpkin Picking Festival! Every fall, children from all over come to ride the hay wagon which Small Fred the Tractor pulls over the hill to his pumpkin patch. The people pick their pumpkins, and Small Fred pulls them back to the farm stand for refreshments and games.

"It must be fun to watch the children try to guess the big pumpkin's weight or find their way through the hay maze," said Mac. "I wish we had a Pumpkin Picking Festival at Stony Meadow Farm. The hay rides! All the happy children! All the big pumpkins!"

"You will have to bring in the apples to the cider mill," Sibley the Horse reminded. "It's that time of year too, you know."

Mac shuddered. "The apple orchard! UGH!" Mac remembered last fall in the apple orchard. His exhaust stack caught on limbs. His big tires tangled in the branches. Apples fell off the trees when he passed and made him sticky. "Yes, it's that time of year too," sighed Mac.

Small Fred had seen the "Apple Time" sign go up across the road at Stony Meadow Farm. "Oh, no – it must also be time for the Pumpkin Picking Festival," Small Fred said to Pepper the Cat. "I can barely pull this hay wagon. The pumpkins are too heavy, and the children are too noisy."

"It's not peaceful and quiet like that beautiful apple orchard across the road," Small Fred said.

Pepper meowed, "It's that time of year, Fred."

Tractor Mac wove through the apple trees the following day. "I'm just too big for this small orchard!" he groaned to Sibley. Branches poked his grill and nearly toppled his exhaust stack!

"Apples are a useful crop," said Sibley. "You can make applesauce, apple pies, apple cider, apple vinegar . . . ."

"Okay, okay," said Mac. "It's just that –" **WUMP!** Mac's big tire hit an apple tree. Tractor Mac and Farmer Bill were showered with apples.

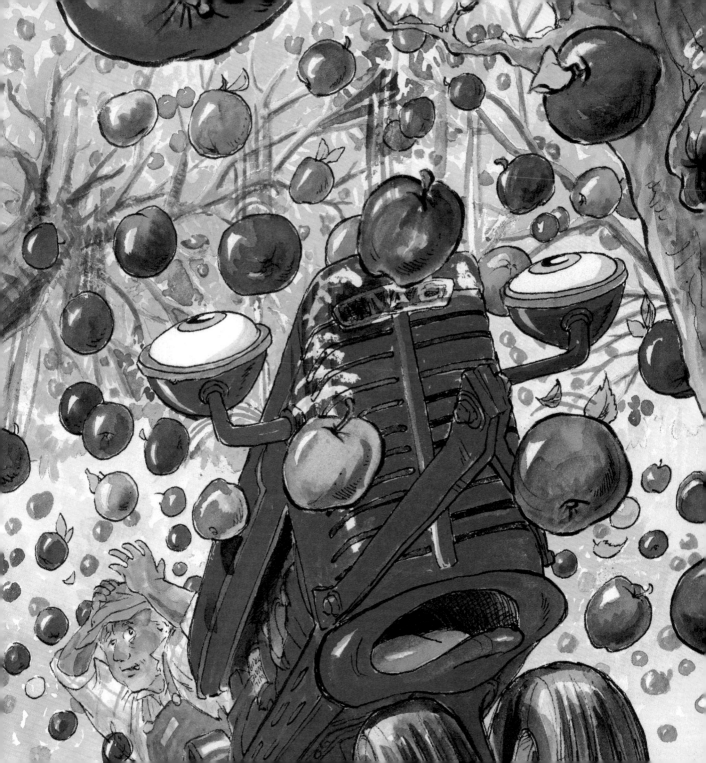

Farmer Bill put Tractor Mac in reverse to back up. **WUMP!** Another apple tree dumped its apples. "Hold on, Mac," laughed Farmer Bill, "or we'll have nothing but applesauce left!"

"You look smashing!" buzzed the bees.

Back at the cider mill, Farmer Bill washed off the apple pulp from Tractor Mac while the big cider press worked away.

"You're not the only one having a hard time today, Mac," said Sam the Ram. "Look at Small Fred over there." Mac could see customers unloading their pumpkins from Fred's wagon. Small Fred couldn't pull the heavy load back over the hill to the farm stand.

"Hmmmm." Farmer Bill said, "You know, a pumpkin patch has much more room to move around in, Mac. I think there may be a better job for a big tractor like you." Mac wheeled down the hill, across the road, and over to where Small Fred sat with his half empty wagon.

Soon Mac was pulling the pumpkin wagon loaded with happy, singing passengers up the hill to the farm stand. "Hooray!" shouted the children.

Small Fred went across the road
to the apple orchard at Stony Meadow Farm.
"You fit perfectly under the apple trees,"
hummed the busy bees.

Small Fred was very happy. It smelled of apples,
and the orchard was peaceful and quiet.

At the end of the day, everyone met back at the Pumpkin Picking Festival. Farmer Bill and Small Fred brought apple cider to share. Small Fred's owner gave Farmer Bill and Tractor Mac the biggest, grandest pumpkin from the pumpkin patch.

CIDER

"I'm glad we could help
each other out," Small Fred said.
"We got to share the work and share
the fun!" said Tractor Mac.